Margaret Hillert's

The Snow Baby

A Beginning-to-Read Book

Illustrated by Laura Krushak–Green

DEAR CAREGIVER,

The books in this Beginning-to-Read collection may look somewhat familiar in that the original versions could have been a part of your own early reading experiences. These carefully written texts feature common sight words to provide your child multiple exposures to the words appearing most frequently in written text. These new versions have been updated and the engaging illustrations are highly appealing to a contemporary audience of young readers.

Begin by reading the story to your child, followed by letting him or her read familiar words and soon your child will be able to read the story independently. At each step of the way, be sure to praise your reader's efforts to build his or her confidence as an independent reader. Discuss the pictures and encourage your child to make connections between the story and his or her own life. At the end of the story, you will find reading activities and a word list that will help your child practice and strengthen beginning reading skills. These activities, along with the comprehension questions are aligned to current standards, so reading efforts at home will directly support the instructional goals in the classroom.

Above all, the most important part of the reading experience is to have fun and enjoy it!

Shannon Cannon

Shannon Cannon,
Literacy Consultant

Norwood House Press • www.norwoodhousepress.com
Beginning-to-Read™ is a registered trademark of Norwood House Press.
Illustration and cover design copyright ©2017 by Norwood House Press. All Rights Reserved.

Authorized adapted reprint from the U.S. English language edition, entitled The Snow Baby by Margaret Hillert. Copyright © 2017 Pearson Education, Inc. or its affiliates. Reprinted with permission. All rights reserved. Pearson and The Snow Baby are trademarks, in the US and/or other countries, of Pearson Education, Inc. or its affiliates. This publication is protected by copyright, and prior permission to re-use in any way in any format is required by both Norwood House Press and Pearson Education. This book is authorized in the United States for use in schools and public libraries.

Designer: Lindaanne Donohoe
Editorial Production: Lisa Walsh

LIBRARY OF CONGRESS CATALOGING-IN-PUBLICATION DATA
Names: Hillert, Margaret, author. I Krushak-Green, Laura, illustrator.
Title: The snow baby / by Margaret Hillert ; illustrated by Laura Krushak-Green.
Description: Chicago, IL : Norwood House Press, 2016. I Series: A beginning-to-read book I Summary: Two children play in the snow and find a furry surprise. Includes reading activities and a word list. I Description based on print version record and CIP data provided by publisher; resource not viewed.
Identifiers: LCCN 2016020724 (print) I LCCN 2016001868 (ebook) I ISBN 9781603579667 (eBook) I ISBN 9781599538044 (library edition : alk. paper)
Subjects: I CYAC: Snow--Fiction.
Classification: LCC PZ7.H558 (print) I LCC PZ7.H558 Sn 2016 (ebook) I DDC [E]--dc23
LC record available at https://lccn.loc.gov/2016020724

288N—072016
Manufactured in the United States of America in North Mankato, Minnesota.

Come here.
Oh, come here.
See it snow.
Down, down, down it comes.

Snow, snow, snow.
See it snow.
We want to play in it.
It is fun to play in.

Oh, oh.
I can not find something.
Something red is not here.
Where is it?
I can not play.

Oh, I see it.
Here it is.
My red one is here.
I can play in the snow.

Look, look.
Little ones and big ones.
See the snow come down.
Run, run, run.

We can make snowballs.
Big, big snowballs.
Work, work, work.

Oh, oh.
I want one to go up here.
I can not make it go.

Here, here.
It is too big for you.
I can help you.
We two can make it go up.

Here is a little one.
It can go up here.
We can make something funny.
It is big and funny.

We can make a snow house, too.
Work, work.
Make a big house.

See me.
See me.
It is fun up here.
Come up, up, up.

One, two, three—jump.
We can jump into the snow.
Find me.
Find me.

Oh, my.
You look funny.
I look funny.
It is fun to play in the snow.

Oh, look.
Here is something.
The big one is me.
The little one is you.

And look here.
I see little spots.
One, two, three.
Three little spots in the snow.

Come, come.
We want to see where
the little spots go.
Look here, look here.

I see something.
It is little.
Is it a little snowball?

Oh, it is a baby.
A little snow baby.
Where is the mother?
Can you find the mother?

The mother is not here.
Come, little baby.
Come to me.
You can come to the house.
Away we go.

Mother, Mother.
Here is a little baby.
It can not run in the snow.
It is too little.

It can come into the house.
It can run and play in here.
We want it.
We want the snow baby.

Foundational Skills

In addition to reading the numerous high-frequency words in the text, this book also supports the development of foundational skills.

Phonological Awareness: The /sn/ sound

Sound Substitution: Say the words on the left to your child. Ask your child to repeat the word, changing the first sound to /**sn**/:

tap = snap	more = snore	pack = snack	rip = snip
peak = sneak	rug = snug	sail = snail	juggle = snuggle

Phonics: The letter S

1. Demonstrate how to form the letters **S** and **s** for your child.
2. Have your child practice writing **S** and **s** at least three times each.
3. Ask your child to point to the words in the book that start with the letter **s**.
4. Write down the following words and ask your child to circle the letter **s** in each word:

see	snow	send	yes	salt
sort	kiss	soft	past	bus
less	list	mustard	so	this

Fluency: Echo Reading

1. Reread the story to your child at least two more times while your child tracks the print by running a finger under the words as they are read.
   Ask your child to read the words he or she knows with you.
2. Reread the story, stopping after each sentence or page to allow your child to read (echo) what you have read. Repeat echo reading and let your child take the lead.

Language

The concepts, illustrations, and text help children develop language both explicitly and implicitly.

Vocabulary: Snowy Day

1. Ask your child to draw a picture of him or herself playing outside on a snowy day.
2. Ask your child to point to the objects in the picture and name them.
3. Label the pictures with the words provided by your child.
4. Ask your child to tell a story to go with the picture using the word labels.
5. If your child has trouble drawing the picture, help him or her to come up with a list of words first and then draw a picture to go with them.

Reading Literature and Informational Text

To support comprehension, ask your child the following questions. The answers either come directly from the text or require inferences and discussion.

Key Ideas and Detail

- Ask your child to retell the sequence of events in the story.
- What did the children do when they got outside?

Craft and Structure

- Is this a book that tells a story or one that gives information? How do you know?
- How do you think the kitten felt when it was outside?

Integration of Knowledge and Ideas

- What animals live in cold weather and enjoy snow?
- Can you describe a time when you needed someone to help you?

WORD LIST

The Snow Baby uses the 50 words listed below.

This list can be used to practice reading the words that appear in the text. You may wish to write the words on index cards and use them to help your child build automatic word recognition. Regular practice with these words will enhance your child's fluency in reading connected text.

a	help	not	the
and	here		three
away	house	oh	to
		one(s)	too
baby	I		two
big	in	play	
	into		up
can	is	red	
come(s)	it	run	want
			we
down	jump	see	where
		snow	work
find	little	snowball(s)	
for	look	something	you
fun		spots	
funny	make		
	me		
go	Mother		
	my		

ABOUT THE AUTHOR Margaret Hillert has helped millions of children all over the world learn to read independently. She was a first grade teacher for 34 years and during that time started writing books that her students could both gain confidence in reading and enjoy. She wrote well over 100 books for children just learning to read. As a child, she enjoyed writing poetry and continued her poetic writings as an adult for both children and adults.

Photograph by Glenna Washburn

ABOUT THE ILLUSTRATOR Laura Krushak–Green is an artist and children's illustrator who grew up in rural Iowa. Having graduated from Brigham Young University–Idaho, Laura has always had a love of creating art featuring children and animals. She lives in Utah with her husband and orange cat. www.laurakg.com